ELVIS THE CROCODILE

AussieArk
WOODSLANE PRESS

ELVIS THE CROCODILE

Woodslane Press Pty Ltd
10 Apollo Street
Warriewood, NSW 2102
Email: info@woodslane.com.au
Tel: 02 8445 2300 **Website:** www.woodslanepress.com.au

First published in Australia in 2023 by Woodslane Press
Reprinted 2023

Royalties from the sale of this book go to support Aussie Ark, a not-for-profit organisation dedicated to wildlife conservation.

Original text and publishing consultant Jo Runciman

Design Mike Ellott

NATIONAL LIBRARY OF AUSTRALIA
A catalogue record for this book is available from the National Library of Australia

FSC www.fsc.org MIX Paper | Supporting responsible forestry FSC® C023121

Printed in China by Hang Tai

Cover image: Elvis the Crocodile

Saltwater crocodiles are Australian **reptiles**. This means they are **cold-blooded** and they lay eggs.

Found in northern Australia, they live in the sea and in inland waters, such as rivers and **billabongs**.

You will often find them **basking** in the sun on sandbanks and beaches.

These giant **reptiles** eat mainly fish, but they will eat anything they can catch. They **submerge** themselves near the water's edge, waiting for their **prey** to come close enough.

This is the story of handsome **Elvis,** Australia's crankiest crocodile!

Elvis used to live in Darwin Harbour, in the Northern Territory of Australia.

He had become a problem because he was **terrorising** people in their boats!

Elvis was so big and handsome, they tried to send him to a crocodile farm to **breed**.

But **Elvis** was so cranky, he kept biting all the other crocodiles.

Lucky for Elvis, **The Australian Reptile Park** said they would like to give him a home.

PARK
REPTILE

Elvis was given his own swimming pool and a special **enclosure** – to keep everyone safe!

A special **reptile** team takes care of **Elvis.**

Jake is his main **keeper**.

Elvis has settled into his new home.

His **keepers** know to be very careful around him.

Wherever they are, **Elvis** is always watching them!

Elvis loves his food. Nothing comes between him and his dinner!

Jake and his team need to be careful that **Elvis** doesn't try to make a meal of them!

They keep **Elvis** healthy by giving him a variety of foods.

Elvis likes chicken, rabbit and kangaroo.

As his main keeper, **Jake** loves and respects **Elvis**.

He understands **Elvis** can be dangerous.

Jake works hard to make sure that **Elvis** is well cared for.

Saltwater crocs live in warm, **tropical** regions of Australia.

Elvis's pool needs to be heated and looked after to a high standard.

Crocodiles do not need to eat very much for their energy needs.

Jake and his team **monitor** closely what, and how much, **Elvis** eats.

Elvis is also Australia's naughtiest **crocodile!**

Once, when his keepers were mowing the lawn, he pulled the mower down to the bottom of his pool.

Then he guarded it so the **keepers** couldn't get it back for days!

He has also stolen a pool scoop and chased keepers out of his **enclosure**.

Elvis is a very big **crocodile.**

He is a giant 4.5 metres long and he weighs over 500 kilograms!

Most male **crocodiles** in the wild do not get as big as **Elvis**.

Nobody knows exactly how old **Elvis** is, but his birthday is celebrated every January.

His **keepers** think he is between 50 and 60 years old.

As male **crocodiles** grow, they get into fights protecting their **territory**.

Elvis must have won most of his battles because he has very few scars on his body.

He is too big to be 30 and too pretty to be 80!

Crocodiles wait and watch their **prey**,
so they know the best time to strike.

The keepers at **The Australian Reptile Park**
change where and how Elvis is fed.

This keeps **Elvis** active and makes it easy
for them to see his whole body.

This way they can check if he is healthy and
moving well – without getting too close!

As a special treat, **Elvis** is sometimes given a big side of beef.

He attacks the food like he would in the wild.

He wrestles with it and performs a spectacular death roll.

This helps to keep even the crankiest **crocodile** happy!

Elvis is a favourite at **The Australian Reptile Park.**

Thousands of people come to see him every year.

CROCODILE FACTS

HABITAT

Saltwater crocodiles inhabit mangrove swamps, coastal marshes, and river mouths around the top of Western Australia, the Northern Territory, and Queensland.

They travel as far up stream as they can swim. They take advantage of floods to access areas normally too difficult to reach.

Salties are able to live in the open ocean for periods of time. They will cross large waters to reach new areas. This is why they can be found across South-East Asia, New Guinea, and some of the Pacific Islands.

Crocodiles are very territorial and will attack other crocodiles, animals and people if they come into their territory.

Crocodile attacks on humans take place because people don't respect how dangerous Australia's northern waterways are.

DIET

Saltwater crocodiles are carnivorous. They eat fish, birds and mammals.

Adult crocodiles eat almost anything that comes too close to the water's edge.

Young crocodiles eat smaller fish and insects.

Humans are not a regular part of a large crocodile's diet. But a person at the water's edge looks like any other mammal to a crocodile!

WATCH ELVIS!

Scan the QR code to see a video of Elvis at **The Australian Reptile Park.**

GLOSSARY

basking: to lie in warm sunshine

billabong: a waterhole of still water

breed: to produce a baby or babies

camouflage: take on the colour, shape or texture of surroundings to trick an enemy carnivorous

cold-blooded: sensitive to cold

digestion: how food is broken down in a body

enclosure: land surrounded by a fence to keep something in

hatch: how young emerge from an egg

ingest: to put food into the body

inhabit: to live in a place

keeper: someone whose job it is to look after animals

mangrove: swampy land

marshes: low, wet land like a swamp

monitor: to check, observe and record changes

muscular: having well-developed muscles

prey: an animal hunted or seized for food

reptile: a cold-blooded vertebrate, including creeping, crawling animals such as lizards, snakes, turtles, alligators, and crocodiles

river mouth: part of the river where the water goes into another body of water

snout: an animal's nose and jaw

submerge: put under the surface of the water

territorial: defence of territory or land

territory: an area of land

terrorising: to fill with fear

tropical: humid

vegetation: plant life

vertebrate: having a backbone or spinal column

webbed: digits (toes) connected by a web, as in ducks' feet